בס"ד

Faiga
Finds the Way

by Batsheva Brandeis

Illustrated by Alexander Levitas

In honor of our beloved children:
Myriam Chaya, Frayda Malka & Menachem Mendel

꙳꙳

Sholom & Esther Laine

Faiga Finds the Way

First Edition January 2006
Second Impression January 2009

For my husband and children, may G-d bless them.
Special thanks to Dr. Paul Kaginsky for his botanical expertise,
and to my daughter Chaya for her typing. B.B.

To my little son, Daniel, with love. A.L.

Editor: D. L. Rosenfeld
Layout: Y. Y. Turner

ISBN-13: 978-1-929628-28-5
ISBN-10: 1-929628-28-5
LCCN: 2005930762

HACHAI PUBLISHING
Brooklyn, New York
Tel 718-633-0100 Fax 718-633-0103
www.hachai.com – info@hachai.com

Printed in U.S.A.

Table of Contents

Historical Note

This story takes place in Russia during the reign of Czar Nicholas the First, when young Jewish boys were being forced to leave home, join the Czar's army, and give up their religion.

The soldiers who roamed the country searching for these Jewish children freely helped themselves to food, livestock, and goods belonging to Russian citizens.

Meet the Family

 Faiga Kaufman is an eleven-year-old girl who lives with her family on a small egg and poultry farm on the outskirts of Kiev by the edge of the Golosov Forest, near the Dnieper River.

 Tzireleh is eight years old and wants to do everything that Faiga does.

 Papa Reb Yankel works hard to support his family and give tzedakah to the poor.

 Mama is constantly busy taking care of everyone and always has a smile on her face.

Aunt Taibke is Mama's younger sister who loves to tell stories about their childhood.

 Uncle Getzel is Aunt Taibke's husband. His farm is not far from where Faiga and her family live.

 Chiggy is the Kaufman family's mischievous goat who stirs up some excitement.

Chapter One

The Empty Wallet

"We need some of your delicious babka cakes this week, and your Aunt Teibke does, too," Mama told Faiga one morning. "Four would be just right."

Faiga smiled. She loved to bake for her family. It made her feel so grown up and important.

"Of course, Mama, she answered. "I can start right now."

Faiga finished braiding her thick brown hair and tied a clean apron around her waist.

"I want to help; I'm a good babka maker," begged her little sister, Tzireleh.

Faiga heaved a sigh and rolled her eyes. Last time the eager eight-year-old had "helped," she'd gotten flour all over her clothes and even in her shoes!

"You can watch," she said firmly. "Come on."

Faiga carefully gathered the ingredients from the pantry: a burlap sack of flour, a basket of eggs, small jars of honey and oil, salt, cinnamon and yeast, a large mixing bowl, and two well-worn wooden spoons.

"Do you really want to help me?" she suddenly asked her little sister.

Tzireleh nodded with excitement.

"Then carry all this out to the table."

The little girl's lower lip began to tremble. Faiga knew she'd gone too far. In another minute there would be tears and tattling.

"I didn't mean it, silly." Faiga said. "We'll do it together. Then I'll let you mix."

As quickly as she'd been ready to cry, Tzireleh's face shone with joy. Faiga sighed again. It was so easy to be perfectly happy when you were only eight. Eleven-year-olds had so much more to worry about.

Together, Faiga and Tzireleh carried the supplies outside to their long wooden table.

With baby Mendeleh in one arm, Mama brought them a pitcher of warm water for the dough.

"Don't waste, and don't spill," she told the girls.

"We'll be careful," Faiga assured her mother.

"Did you remember the honey?"

"Yes, Mama."

Mama smiled. Faiga smiled. Tzireleh smiled. When little Mendeleh gave a toothless grin, Mama laughed and went inside to put him down for a nap.

"Mama always seems so happy," Tzireleh whispered to Faiga.

"I know," Faiga answered. And it was true. Faiga couldn't remember ever seeing Mama without a smile on her face... even last night.

Faiga closed her eyes, thinking about what happened...

* * *

It had been late when Papa came home from shul. Of all the children, only Faiga had been awake when there was a knock at the door.

She'd peeked out curiously from behind the curtain that hid the bed she shared with

Tzireleh. Why would guests be arriving at this late hour?

When Papa had answered the door, there stood a short, elderly man who often came to visit.

Papa had greeted the guest with a voice full of pleasure.

"Rabbi Glick! It's wonderful to see you!"

While Papa made the rabbi comfortable, Mama put the kettle on the fire. Faiga lay back on her soft down pillow and listened.

"Reb Yankel, you can probably guess why I'm here," the rabbi began.

"I'm sure I can," Papa had answered. "Good news always brings you to our home. It must be a wedding!"

Faiga sat upright, and the bed gave a little creak. *A wedding! Was the rabbi going to invite them all to a wedding?*

Rabbi Glick sighed. "Poor girl – she lost her parents to illness. She's alone in the world with no one to pay for even the simplest wedding celebration, or to set her up with household goods."

Faiga heard Mama open the large chest in the corner of the room.

"Here, Rabbi Glick," Mama had said. "I embroidered this tablecloth, stitch by stitch, for the day my Faiga would become a kallah. Thank G-d, I have time to make another. Please take this with my blessings for the poor motherless girl!"

Faiga heard Papa's footsteps approaching her bed. She lay very still and closed her eyes. Papa slowly inched his arm under the mattress, then gently pulled something out from underneath.

From between her half-closed lashes, Faiga peered into the darkness.

Papa lit a candle, and Faiga recognized exactly what he was holding. It was what they always called, "the esrog wallet."

All year long, whenever her mother earned some money from selling eggs, or

Frantically, she groped around for the tzedakah wallet. She'd seen Mama reach for it countless times when a poor traveler came asking for help. Where was it? Faiga started to panic, pushing handkerchiefs out of the way and feeling for the wallet... where was it?

At last! As her fingers touched the worn leather of the tzedakah wallet, Faiga's heart was pounding. She fumbled to open it, lifting the thin leather flap.

All she had to do was slide the money out from behind the curtain. Papa would surely see it and realize his mistake...

Faiga stuck her hand in the wallet, then drew it out in disbelief. Her throat felt so tight and dry that it hurt. *Empty... how could the tzedakah wallet be empty?*

Suddenly her knees grew wobbly, and Faiga sat down on the cold wooden floor. She didn't understand...

"Faiga," It was Mama's voice. "What are you doing on the cold floor?"

Mama stopped and looked from Faiga's white face to the empty wallet lying beside her.

"Back to bed," she said.

Without thinking, Faiga held out her arms like when she was little, and Mama helped her up. Then she tucked her daughter in and sat beside her, stroking Faiga's forehead until the bewildered girl stopped shivering.

Mama picked up the empty tzedakah wallet and placed it back in the top drawer.

"Faiga," she said softly, "I know how you love the mitzvah of lulov and esrog..."

Tears began to roll down Faiga's cheeks. She said, between sobs, "...and the guests who come... and they stay for cake... and I get to be the one who hands them the esrog..."

Mama began to sing a lullaby. It was the same one she sang when Faiga was a baby, and Tzireleh, too. It was the same song she always sang to put little Mendeleh to sleep... *Roizenkes mit Mandlen.*

Faige felt the tightness in her throat let go. She hiccupped a few times, and took a long shuddering breath.

Mama finished her song, and gave her oldest daughter a serious look.

"Faiga, you're old enough to remember when the czar's soldiers were here in the spring."

Faiga remembered. The rough men had ridden through on horseback, looking for young Jewish boys to capture and take to the czar's army. Everyone was relieved when they left without finding a single child!

Mama continued. "They took some of our best hens and grabbed all the eggs they wanted for their meals... all without paying."

Faiga lifted her chin defiantly. "But that's not fair! Why should they take *our* chickens and eggs without paying for them? They're no better than thieves!"

"Hush, maideleh." Mama looked around fearfully. "You mustn't say such things. The czar expects all of us to give his soldiers whatever they want as a way to show our loyalty. Asking to be paid would just make trouble."

Faiga lowered her eyes. "So that's why Papa's wallets are not as full as always."

Mama nodded and smiled bravely. "When the money in the tzedakah wallet had all been given to the poor, your father had to take from the esrog wallet for tzedakah."

"But Mama," Faiga cried, "that means we can't buy an esrog this year. So, why are you smiling?"

Mama held Faiga's hand gently. "Don't you see, maideleh? Your father would rather use Uncle Getzel's lulov and esrog than miss the chance to make a poor kallah happy. How can I not smile when I think of that?"

Faiga had smiled then, too. And when she slept, she dreamt of a kallah holding a basket full of esrogim...

*　*　*

Faiga had been so busy thinking of last night's disappointment, that she didn't notice something cold dripping on her shoes! It was the water pitcher! Tzireleh had knocked it over with her elbow. What a mess!

Impatiently, Faiga moved all the ingredients away from the puddle spreading across the table.

"Tzireleh, why don't you go into the house with the baby and let me finish?"

The second she said it, Faiga knew she'd gone too far again. Tzireleh didn't start to cry this time. She just looked so hurt, so wounded.

"I mean, why don't you move to a dry spot and let me get more water?"

Sighing and sloshing in her wet shoes, Faiga made her way to the well.

As she walked, Faiga couldn't stop thinking of the empty esrog wallet.

"Wouldn't Papa be surprised and happy if I found a way to earn enough money for an esrog!" she thought. "But how?"

Suddenly, Faiga had an idea.

I could sell babka cakes! Mine are as good as any I've ever tasted... except Mama's. I'll start today! Instead of four cakes, I'll bake more and sell the extra ones in town!

Chapter Two

Faiga's Plan

Without wasting a moment, Faiga filled the pitcher with well water and hiked back to begin her baking. She was hoping Tzireleh would have lost interest by now and have disappeared into the house.

I want my extra babkas to be my own special surprise. Won't the whole family be amazed when they see I've filled the esrog wallet all by myself!

As she came closer to the table, Faiga saw that Tzireleh was still there, waiting patiently. *Why couldn't her little sister ever leave her alone?*

"Faiga," she said, "I'm sorry for spilling. May I have some of that water for Chiggy? He looks thirsty."

Faiga glanced over at Chiggy, their mischievous, dark-brown mountain goat.

They always treated her well, never forgetting that their family needed her rich goat's milk for their breakfast and for making the salty cheese they all loved.

"I guess everyone spills sometimes," Faiga answered. "Take as much water as you need; I've got to get to work."

Faiga began measuring the ingredients and pouring them into the bowl. She loved watching the messy mixture of water, yeast, eggs, oil and honey blend into a golden syrup. Next she added the flour, bit by bit, mixing until every lump disappeared.

In her mind, she could picture the ladies in town standing in line to buy her beautiful babkas.

They would say: "Have you ever smelled anything so delicious?" "I'd like to order a dozen more, please." "Who is the excellent baker who made these?"

Faiga smiled; she could almost feel the esrog wallet, heavy with coins.

She mixed the dough for an extra long time, until it grew smooth and round.

"Can I help?" Tzireleh's voice broke into her thoughts. "You didn't let me do anything!"

Faiga sighed noisily. "All right, wet this cloth and cover the dough. That will help it rise."

The little girl happily dampened a clean cloth and placed it over the bowl.

Before long, the mound of dough began pushing up against the cloth. Faiga punched it down a few times and let it rise again.

A short time later, Mama came out to check on them. "Why girls, it's nice to see the two of you working together so nicely. That dough looks beautiful!"

Faiga bit her lip. They hadn't been working together, not really.

She and Tzireleh watched as Mama made the brachah, "L'hafrish Challah," and took off a small piece of dough.

"Amein," they answered. Then Mama took the piece back into the house to burn.

Faiga divided the fresh, springy dough into seven chunks, pressed each one into a flat triangle shape, and began to drizzle honey, oil, and cinnamon over the tops.

Of course Tzireleh noticed the extra babkas. "What are you doing, Faiga? Why do we need so many?"

"I have my reasons," Faiga replied mysteriously. "Now move over so I can roll up the dough."

Tzireleh looked at her with wide pleading eyes, but Faiga was not about to let her little sister ruin this special batch of cakes. *These had to be perfect... they just had to! Tzireleh would be happy when she saw this year's esrog, wouldn't she?*

Carefully, Faiga shaped each babka cake into a nice tight roll and smoothed more oil over the tops. She wiped her hands and stepped back to admire her handiwork. They did look perfect!

"I'm going in to get the baking pans; you watch over the dough."

Faiga couldn't help smiling as she ran into the house. Her heart felt light and free. How proud Papa and Mama would be that she could solve the esrog problem all by herself!

Quietly, so as not to disturb the baby, Faiga took out the heavy metal baking pans. She wiped and coated each one with oil so the babkas wouldn't stick and burn.

Suddenly, there was a cry from outside. It was Tzireleh, shouting and calling loudly enough to wake Mendeleh.

"What now?" thought Faiga, shaking her head. She picked up the heavy pans and stepped outside.

An awful sight met her eyes!

Chiggy, had gotten out of her pen. Of course, the hungry animal headed straight for the sweet-smelling babkas lined up on the table!

"Tzireleh!" yelled Faiga angrily. "Get that goat away from my babkas!"

"I'm trying," answered Tzireleh tearfully. She pulled Chiggy with all her might, but her eight-year-old arms were no match for the determined goat.

"Shoo! Get away!" yelled Faiga. She banged the metal pans together and chased the goat back into her pen. "Tzireleh, latch the gate!"

Her little sister closed the pen and sat down right there on the grass with her head in her hands. Faiga went over to the table to see what damage had been done.

Three babkas were gone; Chiggy had gobbled every bit of them. One lay in the dirt under the table, completely ruined. Only three babkas remained on the table, squashed and out of shape.

"Three babkas," she whispered. "There aren't even enough for us and for Aunt Taibke."

Mama came out of the house and put her hand on Faiga's shoulder.

"Oh, maideleh," she said softly, "zol zein a kaparah. Better something should happen to those babkas than to my precious children."

Faiga buried her head in Mama's dress. Of course her mother would say that! She didn't know about the secret plan.

She lifted her head. "Mama, may I bake more?"

Mama sighed. "I wouldn't mind if you did, but we're running low on supplies. I'll need the flour for challah this week."

Faiga looked surprised. "But why can't we buy more flour in town?"

Mama avoided Faiga's eyes. "We already have a big bill at the store in town. As soon as we pay it, we'll buy everything we need."

Mama hugged her and smiled. Faiga smiled back, but now she had a new, more serious worry. She hadn't realized Mama and Papa didn't even have money to buy flour and other supplies. What if they didn't have enough food for the winter ahead?

Faiga walked over to the table. She would have to try to fix the smashed babkas the best she could. Tzireleh walked over and stood next to her.

"I'm sorry, Faiga," she said in a small voice. "It was just a mistake."

Faiga glared at her sister. *This was really all Tzireleh's fault! If she had just latched that gate, none of this would have happened! Little children and goats were just a big nuisance. They spoiled everything!*

Faiga picked up the raw, dirty babka from under the table. She threw it into Chiggy's pen, and the goat quickly finished it off.

Faiga glared at Chiggy, too. She turned and placed the lopsided babkas on a pan and went to put them into the oven.

Tears of disappointment filled her eyes. Without enough flour, the whole surprise plan would never have worked anyway. Buying an esrog seemed impossible now. Wasn't there anything she could do to help her family?

* * *

That night, after Tzireleh said 'Shema' and snuggled down under the covers, she added an extra tefillah out loud.

"Please, Hashem, help Faiga forgive me for what happened to the babkas."

Faiga, who had had been getting ready for bed, popped her head out of her nightgown and looked over at her little sister.

Tzireleh was tucked under the patchwork quilt, her blond curls spread out on the pillow behind her. The little girl was trying her best to keep her eyes closed, peeking every few seconds to check if Faiga was watching.

Faiga grinned. It was easy to get upset at Tzireleh, but hard to stay that way.

"Hashem has answered you! You are forgiven, but I'm still a little angry at Chiggy."

Tzireleh sat up and giggled. "You did look kind of funny running out of the house and banging on those pans."

Both girls collapsed with laughter. They made such a racket that Mama had to come in twice to quiet them down.

"It's late, girls. Try to get some sleep. Tomorrow, I want you to go into the woods and gather blackberries for jelly."

Faiga licked her lips. Mama's blackberry jelly was her favorite!

Suddenly, Faiga had an idea.

"Tzireleh, can you work extra hard tomorrow and gather enough berries for Mama by yourself?"

The little girl wrinkled her forehead. "And why should I do all the work? Where will you be?"

"Me, too," Tzireleh said. She tied her kerchief under her chin.

Their mother bent down and looked into their eyes. "Now remember, stay together, don't get lost, and be back in time for supper."

"We will, Mama," they chorused.

Faiga sighed with contentment. A slight breeze was blowing, rustling the leaves above them. From all sides came the chirping of birds and the song of the crickets.

"Hurry up, Tzireleh," said Faiga. "Why are you always slow?"

"Sorry," the little girl replied. "It's just these shoes."

She sighed. "They used to be yours, but they're still too big for me. And this hole on the side keeps letting little stones in."

Faiga bit her lip. She shouldn't have called Tzireleh slow. It wasn't her fault that she couldn't have decent shoes. Faiga looked down at her own worn pair. They used to be Mama's; at least they had no holes.

If I sell all the berries I pick today, will I have enough for an esrog, enough for the grocery bill, and enough for a new pair of shoes for Tzireleh? Faiga didn't think so.

Lost in her daydreams, Faiga missed the path toward the berry bushes. She kept walking, with Tzireleh lagging a few steps behind.

"Faiga," called her little sister. "This isn't the way we went last time."

Faiga looked around with a start. "Just follow me; I know what I'm doing."

She didn't want Tzireleh to get scared, so Faiga kept on going as if she were on the right path. "I think we're close now."

"You *think*?" Tzireleh narrowed her eyes. "What do you mean, 'you *think*?' Does that mean you don't *know*?"

Faiga didn't answer. She kept going more deeply into the forest, certain that she'd find her way back to the path if she could just recognize some landmarks.

"All we need to do is find the big rock at the edge of the stream," said Faiga. "It's shaped like a triangle... it's right around here," she added softly, "I think."

Faiga was starting to panic. Every tree looked the same; the path was nowhere in sight.

After twenty more minutes of tramping through the forest, Tzireleh began to cry.

"You're going too fast. I can't walk anymore. Where are the berry bushes? I'm hungry. I'm thirsty, too."

Faiga looked back at Tzireleh. The little girl's face was smudged with streaks of dirt and sweat. Her blond braids were coming loose, and her sleeve had caught on a branch and ripped.

This was bad... very bad. Papa had always told her that if she got lost in the forest to *stay put*. She'd been walking around in circles for so long, what if no one could find them?

Faiga knew one thing. She had to take care of her sister, no matter what. She didn't need a crying eight-year-old on her hands.

"Let's rest for a bit, Tzireleh. Come sit over here by these purple flowers. I'll pick some to put in your hair."

The thought of wearing wildflowers in her hair brought a smile to the little girl's face.

"You're the best sister – the best! You know what I'll do? I'll make a bouquet for Mama," she said brightly. "Won't she like that, Faiga?"

"Of course," the older girl answered. "She'll just love it."

Faiga forced herself to sit down and think calmly. She said a kapital Tehillim that she knew by heart, and whispered, "Please, Hashem, help me get out of this mess."

She began whispering to herself. "I know we need to go toward the river. I know the path goes by the big rock. I know the big rock is near a hill. How can I see where I am with all these trees? These trees are blocking my view."

Her eyes filled with tears. "All these trees are in the way... trees, trees, trees... wait! That's it!"

Faiga jumped to her feet and looked around. Then she dashed to the tallest chestnut tree with the strongest branches, and began to climb. Higher and higher she went, hope growing in her heart.

"If I can just see the hill, I'll know the river is beyond!"

Tzireleh's voice drifted up. "Faiga, why are you climbing that tree? Faiga, can I climb with you?"

Panting with the effort, she continued to climb, reaching for one branch after the other. At last, Faiga poked her head up above the leafy canopy of the forest. To her right lay a clearing, and just a stone's throw from there, was the hill!

She smiled a triumphant smile and mouthed the words, "Thank You, Hashem!" Then she called down, "I just felt like climbing this tree, and no, you can't climb with me until you're older. Now, do you want to pick some berries or not?"

Tzireleh nodded, "Let's go!" She looked like a little princess with purple flowers stuck into her blond braids.

The two girls made their way to the clearing, past the hill, and on through the forest to the stream with the triangle rock. It seemed to point the way to the bushes, laden with sweet, plump blackberries.

For the next few hours, the two sisters worked happily, eating berries, putting the very best ones in their baskets. Their tongues turned purple; their fingers grew scratched and sticky. They were completely absorbed in their task, Tzireleh thinking of Mama's blackberry jelly, Faiga imagining over and over again how selling her berries would save her family from their problems.

Hours passed. Tzireleh took off her apron, lay down to rest, and fell asleep. Faiga worked on, filling her basket fuller than ever before, thinking, "This is how full the esrog wallet will be!"

Her neck grew stiff; her back began to ache, but still Faiga continued. Crickets chirped lazily, and birds called to each other in the tall branches overhead.

Suddenly, the forest grew still and quiet. It was startling, really, how nothing moved or made a sound.

Faiga looked up, puzzled for a moment, until she saw the angry gray sky and felt the wind pick up. It looked like a heavy rainstorm was coming.

Just a few seconds later, Faiga heard the first fat drops hit the leaves. The berries! Quickly, Faiga dashed to bring both baskets of berries to a protected spot under the nearest chestnut tree.

Large branches spread out above her, creating what felt like a shelter from the storm.

"Tzireleh, wake up! A storm's coming. Let's wait it out under the tree with our berries. These strong rains don't usually last long."

Tzireleh yawned, stretched, and frowned. She folded her arms and answered, "No! Papa said never to stay under a tree in a storm. I won't!"

Faiga could feel the blood rise in her face and her temples start to pound. "That's only if there's thunder and lightening."

"I won't," Tzireleh yelled.

"Stubborn child," Faiga muttered darkly. She marched into the downpour to grab her sister's arm and pull her away from the clearing.

"You're getting soaked. You come with me, or when we get home, I'll..."

There was no time to finish the thought. At that instant, a huge flash lit up the clearing, followed by a harsh cracking sound. Faiga watched open-mouthed, as the mighty tree crashed to the forest floor, barely missing the two girls.

Instinctively, Faiga fell to the ground, pulling Tzireleh down next to her. With rain drenching their hair and soaking their clothes, they lay there – breathless, shocked by their narrow escape.

Neither of them knew how long they remained in that position, afraid to lift their heads, too limp to move.

Faiga hugged Tzireleh close, and tears poured from beneath her closed eyelids, mingling with the rain. If Tzireleh had listened to her, they both would have been right under the tree when it came down. They both could have been severely injured, or worse.

At last the sky grew lighter... the rain softer... until it stopped completely. The nightmare was over.

Faiga couldn't seem to find her voice. She sat up and looked back at the massive tree, lying across the clearing. Their baskets had overturned, and crushed berries were everywhere.

Stiffly, Faiga held out her hand to help Tzireleh get up. The little girl was shivering from cold and fear. Her teeth chattered, and her thin cotton dress clung to her body.

"Where's your apron? Oh, never mind. We've got to get you warm and dry. Come on."

"Faiga, I hear water, we must be near the river." They stopped and listened. Which way was it coming from? The girls were so thoroughly drenched that Faiga didn't want to think about water, especially a whole river-full.

Then she remembered Feivish's shed. It was a storage hut that an elderly handyman used for his fishing equipment, tools, and all kinds of other junk. It was right between the edge of the forest and the river.

Faiga felt relief wash over her as she hurried her sister along. *Feivish must be out on a job, but surely he won't mind if we sit inside to warm up.*

Chapter Four

Roizenkes mit Mandlen

Together, they ran towards the weathered wooden structure. Their relief at reaching the shed quickly turned to dismay upon realizing that the door wouldn't budge. Faiga held back her tears while pulling at the handle as hard as she could.

"Why isn't it opening?" chattered Tzireleh.

"Because when wood gets wet, it swells. This door is stuck. We have to find another door or a window." Faiga slid through the mud to the other side of the shed.

"Here's an open window. Hurry," commanded Faiga.

They climbed carefully on an upside down boat. Faiga clasped her hands together so that Tzireleh could put one foot in and get a boost up to the window. Tzireleh climbed through the opening and onto something that felt like a pile of wood.

Tzireleh watched to see how Faiga would get in. "Where are you going?" Tzireleh shouted.

"I'm looking for a crate," answered Faiga. On the side of the shed was a box that served as a chair when Feivish mended his fishnets. Faiga balanced it on the boat, hoisted herself up, and joined her sister in the dark, crowded hut.

Just a few minutes later, rain began to pound on the roof. They had made it just in time!

Faiga searched through piles of odds and ends until she found a woolen blanket.

"This is for you," she said to Tzireleh. "We've got to get you warmed up."

Tenderly, Faiga wrapped her younger sister in the heavy blanket. Tzireleh lay back and closed her eyes. Only then did Faiga realize that she herself was shaking with cold and shock.

A dirty piece of canvas covered Feivish's tools. Faiga lifted one end and draped it over her shoulders for warmth.

Faiga put her head in her hands. What a disaster this turned out to be! Mama would be so worried. As the rain drummed on the roof, Faiga thought about the events of the day. She pictured herself setting off that morning, full of hope and excitement. Now everything was spoiled... everything.

"Faiga," her little sister called.

"What?"

"How long will we have to wait here?"

"Until this rain stops. Now close your eyes again."

"I can't. I'm afraid of spiders. And my arm is all itchy."

Faiga sighed. "I don't see any spiders. Your arm is probably itchy from the blanket. Here, let me see."

She examined Tzireleh's arm closely in the dim light. Small, red blotches were visible near her wrist. Faiga let out a groan.

"Tzireleh, this looks like poison ivy! Don't scratch, or you're going to have it all over."

"But it itches! I can't help it!"

Faiga glanced around the shed for something, anything, to help her sister.

"I know. Reach up and stick your arm out the window. The rain will feel good on the itchy part."

Tzireleh stood with one arm out the window, bravely trying not to cry.

"Can we go home already?" she begged.

"As soon as the rain lets up a little, we'll go home."

"This rain is never going to stop!" Tears rolled down Tzireleh's cheeks.

Faiga felt miserable. After all, she was the one responsible for Tzireleh. Why had she let her fall asleep under that tree? That must have been where the poison ivy was.

And how could she have forgotten the rule about not standing under a tree during a storm? Why, even an eight-year-old had known better than that!

Between the rain pounding on the roof, the distant thunder, and Tzireleh's sobbing, Faiga thought she would start crying herself.

Instead, she began humming Mama's familiar song that comforted children of all ages:

"*Roizenkes mit mandlen...*" Faiga put her arm around Tzireleh's shoulders. "Sing with me." At first Tzireleh's voice quavered, but soon the two sisters were swaying and singing together. Their voices grew stronger, and the louder they sang, the better they felt.

All at once, Faiga put her finger over her sister's lips. "Quiet! I just heard something."

They strained their ears to hear over the sounds of the storm.

"Faaaiga! Tziiiireleh!"

"Someone's calling our names," exclaimed Tzireleh. "It's Papa!"

"Papa! Papa!" Faiga and Tzireleh bumped heads as they looked out the window together. Holding a small wooden board over his head, their father slogged through the wet grass, searching for them.

"Papa! We're in here!" Faiga and Tzireleh shouted.

Papa was dripping wet, running and gasping with relief.

"Maidelach," he cried hoarsely. "I saw the tree... the baskets of berries... and this... crushed underneath..." He held up Tzireleh's apron. "And I thought... for one terrible moment, I thought..."

He reached in through the window of the shed, and a moment later, Tzireleh was in his arms. Faiga was next to climb out. The knot in her stomach began to ease as she realized her strong, capable father was in charge now. He hugged them both as if he would never let go.

"Baruch Hashem," he whispered.

Faiga buried her face in his shoulder. Her throat felt tight and sore. "Papa," she whispered, "I'm sorry you had to come and get us in the rain."

"How did you find us?" Tzireleh asked.

"I walked on the path toward the berry bushes, and followed the river's edge this way. After I saw the fallen tree in the clearing,

I noticed Feivish's shed in the distance. I ran closer and closer, when suddenly, I heard a familiar tune..."

"That was Faiga's idea," Tzireleh said. "She started singing to me."

Tatte's eyes twinkled. "When I heard you singing Mama's lullaby, I knew where you were."

Thunder rumbled in the distance. Papa stopped hugging them and looked up at the sky.

"We'd better go quickly. This storm's not over yet."

He picked up Tzireleh, dripping wet, and wrapped her in his warm coat.

"Faiga, are you alright? Can you walk home?"

Faiga nodded and sloshed along the muddy trail behind her father, struggling to keep up with his long strides. Her feelings were all mixed up in a jumble.

She had never felt so grateful to be alive, so disappointed that her plan ended in failure. She felt so happy that Tzireleh was safe in her father's arms, so ashamed that she hadn't taken better care of her younger sister.

Tears stung her eyelids. Every time she tried to help her family, things went horribly wrong. How could she have ever thought she could raise enough money for an esrog or a pair of shoes or anything else?

Well, that's it, Faiga decided. *No more plans, no more surprises, no more bright ideas... I give up.*

* * *

Back home, Mama wasted no time drying them off and bustling them both into thick flannel nightgowns. She threw warm shawls over their shoulders, put a cooling salve on Tzireleh's rash, and served the girls steaming cups of peppermint tea.

Tzireleh couldn't stop talking, eager to share every aspect of their adventure with Mama. The more she talked, the worse Faiga felt. She couldn't look Mama in the eye.

At last, Tzireleh grew quiet, and Faiga realized that the little girl had fallen asleep right in her chair. She looked over at her little sister. What a day they'd had together!

A few soggy purple flowers were still stuck in her blond hair. Faiga gently plucked them out as Mama carried Tzireleh off to bed.

A moment later, Mama came back and pulled Faiga onto her lap. "Now, would you like to tell me about it?"

Suddenly, Faiga realized that she would. She started at the very beginning and told Mama everything... her first idea to sell babkas... her second idea to sell berries...

"I just can't imagine a Yom Tov without all the supplies we need," Faiga said tearfully, "and without a beautiful esrog."

She looked down at the purple flowers in her hand. "I'm sorry, Mama. I just wanted to fix everything. But I guess I can't do anything right."

Mama cupped Faiga's chin and looked into her eyes. "Yom Tov is about much more than the special foods we eat or being able to afford a nice esrog," she said.

"We have a whole month of holidays to make us think and grow. Rosh Hashanah is about crowning Hashem as our King... and about new beginnings. Yom Kippur is about doing teshuvah, about forgiveness... Sukkos is about relying on Hashem alone... Simchas Torah is about serving Him with joy."

Faiga thought about that while Mama held her close.

"You still look upset," Mama said, breaking the silence.

Faiga hesitated. "How can I forget that I put Tzireleh in danger during the storm? I was supposed to be watching her, and then she got poison ivy. I'm so sorry. Will you ever trust me again?"

Mama smiled. "Teshuvah doesn't mean forgetting our mistakes, but feeling sorry about what happened and learning for the future. I know you regret the mistakes you made today, but you did so many wonderful and brave things today, too."

Faiga looked up, surprised.

"You found a warm, dry place for yourself and your sister. You figured out a way to get in and wrapped her in a warm blanket. You were smart enough to wash and cool her rash with the rain. You comforted her with a song just as I would have done."

Faiga's eyes grew brighter, and she smiled for the first time since the morning.

"So you see," Mama said, as she led Faiga to her bed and tucked her in, "it's time to stop blaming yourself and to continue on with joy. If you ask me, there's no one I trust more than my Faiga!"

Chapter Five
A New Beginning

It was odd to wake up with the sun already high in the sky. Mama had done their morning chores so the girls could sleep late and recover from their ordeal.

Faiga said 'Modeh Ani' and washed quickly next to her bed. On a chair nearby lay her dress and apron, all clean and starched.

Mama came in smiling. "Get up, you two!" Tzireleh murmured 'Modeh Ani' and washed, too. Her hand and wrist were still bandaged because of the poison ivy rash underneath.

Yesterday, looking at that bandage had made Faiga's heart ache with sadness and shame. Today, she felt eager to fix things... to make this new day just as wonderful as could be.

"Tzireleh, do you need any help buttoning your dress?"

"Thank you, Faiga," replied the little girl. "It's hard for me to reach the middle ones by myself."

After Faiga helped her sister dress and braid her hair, she slipped on her own clothes. Looking down, she noticed the purple flowers from last night, lying forgotten on the floor. Faiga picked them up and cheerfully pinned them on her collar.

"Yom Tov will still be special," she said out loud, "...no matter what we have or what we don't."

Faiga entered the kitchen just as Mama was unwrapping the bandage from Tzireleh's hand. "Does it still bother you, maideleh?"

"Not too much," Tzireleh answered. "It's just itchy; that's all."

Mama reached for the jar of salve, took off the lid, and shook her head.

"I don't have nearly enough of this left," she said, scraping the bottom of the jar. With a clean cloth, she bandaged Tzireleh's hand, then let out a deep sigh.

"What is it, Mama?" Faiga asked.

"I need to make more of this cooling salve for Tzireleh. Without it, she'll start to scratch and the rash may spread."

Anxious to be useful, Faiga took the jar from her mother's hands. "Just tell me what to do," she said. "I'll make more for Tzireleh."

Mama smiled. "I know you mean well, Faiga, but to make this salve I need some herbs from Shaya's spice shop in town. I won't be able to pay him today, but if he lets us put it on our bill..."

"You're going to town?" asked Tzireleh. "Can I come, too?"

"I can't spend the day in town," Mama answered, "there's too much to do here today, and the baby is fussy."

As if he understood her words, Mendeleh began to screech in his cradle.

Faiga stood holding the empty jar, a thoughtful look on her face.

"Mama," she said softly, "I could go."

Mama looked over the top of the baby's head, and her eyes met Faiga's for a brief instant.

"Yes," she said suddenly. "Uncle Getzel and Aunt Taibke will be going today. I don't want to ask them to shop for me... they'll insist on paying for everything. I believe you are the only person to go and pick up the herbs I need. You can stop by at the general store, too."

"Why does Faiga get to go? May I go along?" Tzireleh begged.

Mama smiled at her younger daughter. "You'll have your chance, when that rash is better."

Faiga's face was glowing. *Mama really does trust me! This time, I'll make her proud!*

While Faiga wrapped up some fruit and goat cheese to take along, Mama wrote down the names of the herbs she needed. Faiga tucked the precious note into her apron pocket next to her clean handkerchief.

When she heard her aunt and uncle's wagon pull up in front of the house, Faiga hugged Mama and dashed out the door. Smiling and waving, tall Uncle Getzel held the reins, the midday sun lighting up his orange beard.

Aunt Taibke looked cool and elegant, as always. Her blue eyes twinkled as she motioned for Faiga to climb in and sit next to her.

"Bye, Tzireleh!" called Faiga. "Bye, Mama! Don't worry. I'll be back before you know it, Im Yirtzeh Hashem."

Uncle Getzel clucked gently and gave a soft slap with the reins. Slowly, the wagon began to sway down the dirt road in the direction of town.

The road was still muddy from yesterday's rain, and the fields smelled of fresh earth and growing things.

To pass the time, Aunt Taibke told stories of when she and Mama were young. It was hard for Faiga to believe that her mother was ever a little girl.

"Did you and Mama really eat all those plums and get a stomach ache?"

Aunt Taibke laughed. "We were sick for two days. And neither one of us has been able to eat plums since!"

Faiga laughed, too. Then she turned to her aunt with a serious face.

"Mama is the older sister. Was she nice to you?"

Aunt Taibke looked into Faiga's eyes. "Well, sometimes she seemed very impatient with me. Sometimes she got upset when I ruined her plans. But she always protected me and helped me out. That's how I knew she loved me."

Faiga thought about that. "You know," she confided shyly, "Tzireleh is always tagging along after me, but sometimes I don't mind as much as I used to."

"I'm guessing that the older you get, the closer you and Tzireleh will be," Aunt Taibke said. "Just look at your mother and me; now we're best friends."

Faiga tried to picture herself all grown up with Tzireleh married and living nearby. She shook her head. "I can't imagine that ever happening."

Aunt Taibke laughed again. "Neither could I, but it did!"

As time passed, Faiga grew hot and tired. She nibbled the food that she'd brought, and the goat cheese made her very thirsty. Finally, Faiga saw the small town in the distance.

At last Uncle Getzel brought the wagon to a stop at the well. He poured some water in the trough for the horses, then filled a large dipper and handed it to Faiga. She made a brachah and took a long, wet gulp. The well water felt deliciously cold as it slid down her parched throat.

Uncle Getzel smiled down at her. "Why don't you look around in the shops while we tie up the horses?"

"Are you sure you don't need any help?" Faiga asked.

"Go on," answered her aunt. "We'll meet up with you soon."

Faiga was off in a flash. It had been months since she'd been in town, and she couldn't wait to visit the general store.

She made her way up the wooden steps and into the crowded shop. She picked her way past barrels of flour and crates of tools. The shelves were packed with bolts of cloth, delicate lace, toys and trinkets, food supplies and candy. Behind a glass case was her favorite display of ladies' gloves and fans. Faiga hardly knew where to look first.

"What can I do for you today, young lady?" The owner of the store beamed at Faiga.

"Here's my mother's list," she replied with a smile.

"Hmmmm, you need flour, some nails, and a length of strong rope. Will you be putting that on the bill?"

Faiga nodded, but her heart sank. Mama and Papa had asked for so few things. There would be no cloth for new dresses this year...

no white sugar for baking, no shiny hair ribbons, and no candy!

"Yom Tov will still be special," she reminded herself, "...no matter what we have or what we don't."

Faiga thanked the store owner, and left carrying her small package. Taking a deep breath, she walked up the wooden steps to Shaya's spice store.

A small bell announced her arrival. Faiga stopped to sniff the pungent, sweet scent of the shop. Bunches of dried plants and flowers hung from the rafters. Rows of glass jars filled the shelves.

One wall was lined from ceiling to floor with tiny wooden drawers, each labeled with the name of its contents: black pepper, bay leaf, paprika. Faiga knew that some spices would be used to season food, while others would be boiled as tea, or prepared as medicine.

Faiga was so busy taking in all the interesting sights and smells, that she didn't notice Shaya's wife, Shaindel, stepping up to the counter.

"Hello Faiga," she said. "I'm so happy to see you here in town."

"I came with my aunt and uncle," Faiga answered shyly. "My mama needs these herbs and sent me to get them."

Sheindel took the paper from Faiga's hand and turned to open one of the little drawers. With a small scoop, she dipped into the drawer and poured the precious herb into a cone of brown paper.

Deftly, she folded the cone in half and tied it around with a small length of string.

"Here you go, Faiga. That will be two kopecks, please."

Faiga gulped and said, "Mama would like you to write it down, please. She said she'll pay you the next time she comes to town."

"That's fine with me," answered the older woman. "But I have a better idea. I'll trade this package of herbs for those hyssop flowers you're wearing on your collar. We're out of hyssop just now and it will be quite a while before we have more."

"Hyssop?" echoed Faiga in surprise. "Is that what these purple flowers are called?"

"That's right," said Sheindel. "And hyssop is good for so many things. It's really quite expensive, because hyssop doesn't normally grow around here."

"What is it good for?" Faiga asked curiously.

"Well, people use it for medicine, tea, perfume... and for making mashke, you know, strong drinks. It was even used in the time of the Bais Hamikdosh!"

Faiga felt her cheeks flush with excitement. "How expensive is it... I mean, if I were able to bring you a great deal of hyssop, how much would it be worth?"

Sheindel's eyes twinkled at her.

"Let's just say we'd pay you enough rubles to make it worthwhile."

Faiga gasped. *Rubles for flowers? Who could ever imagine that?*

"One more thing," she asked. "How do I pick the hyssop, I mean, what part is important... the flower, the roots?"

Shaya's wife smiled at Faiga's eagerness to learn.

"I need the flowers on a long stalk for drying upside down like the plants you see here. But if you dig up the roots and plant them in a special corner of your farm, you'll have enough to grow and sell for years to come!"

Faiga's eyes grew bright with hope. This was the best idea yet! She could just picture Papa buying a beautiful esrog, paying the bill at the general store, bringing home candy and white sugar, and even new shoes for Tzireleh... all because of her hyssop!

"I'll do it!" she blurted out. "I'll come back with stalks of hyssop just as soon as I can!"

Her fingers fumbled to remove the small bunch of purple flowers she had pinned to her dress that morning.

"Thank you so, so much!" she said, as she handed the hyssop to Sheindel.

Faiga practically danced out of the shop, clutching her bundles. She couldn't believe her good fortune. Hashem had shown her the way to help!

Chapter Six
Secrets and Surprises

The wagon swayed back and forth, but Faiga was too excited to close her eyes. She was busy making plans and imagining how she would surprise her family.

Aunt Taibke glanced over at her quizzically. "Faiga, you look so pleased with yourself. You haven't sat still for one minute since we got back into this wagon. What on earth happened to you in town?"

Faiga was bursting to tell someone her wonderful news. But how would Mama feel if she told her aunt and uncle about their troubles? The only reason she had come to town with them was to keep them from offering to pay for everything at the store.

"It's kind of a secret," Faiga answered, "...a good secret... a surprise, really."

Aunt Taibke laughed. "Did I ever tell you about the time your Mama and I were determined to surprise our mother and cook chicken soup for Shabbos? We filled her big soup pot with water, but then it was too heavy for us to lift!"

Her aunt twinkled at her. "Can you guess what we did then?"

Faiga knew the answer. She'd heard this story many times before.

"You ran back and forth filling it up one cup at a time."

Aunt Taibke laughed again. "We spilled so much water in the process that the fire in the fireplace went out, and we knew better than to light it ourselves. That was the end of our chicken soup surprise!"

Faiga smiled, but a niggling little doubt began to grow in her mind. Maybe this whole idea was too hard for her to manage alone. She tried to think of all the details involved.

"I need a wheelbarrow and shovel; that's easy enough. I need something sharp to cut the hyssop... not a knife, maybe a pair of scissors. Then I've got to dig up the roots... where's a safe place to plant them... far away from Chiggy's pen?"

Faiga wrinkled her forehead.

Cutting the hyssop, tying it up, digging out the roots and replanting would take hours! She sighed. She was going to need help; there was no way to surprise everyone.

"Well," she thought, "just because I can't surprise everyone, doesn't mean I can't surprise anyone! Should I tell Mama? She would help me, and we could surprise Papa together!"

Faiga bit her lip. Mama was so busy with the baby, the cooking, the washing, and her vegetable garden. Maybe she should tell Papa instead, and they'd surprise Mama.

"No," she thought. "Papa's chores last all day, and then he learns Torah at night. When would he have the time?"

Faiga slumped down against the seat of the wagon, limp and discouraged. She knew the hyssop would be the answer to her family's problems, but she really wanted to keep it a secret until the money was in her hand!

Lost in thought, Faiga didn't even realize when the wagon pulled up and stopped at her front door.

"Faiga," said Aunt Taibke, "I'm sure your Mama's waiting anxiously for you."

"Thank you so much for taking me," replied Faiga. "I had a lovely time!"

She hugged Aunt Taibke and waved goodbye to her uncle. Clutching her packages, Faiga ran into the house.

* * *

Later that night, after Mama put Mendeleh to sleep, she gently smoothed the healing salve on Tzireleh's rash.

"It's almost better now," Mama smiled. "What a reminder of your adventures. Get to bed girls; tomorrow's another day!"

Tzireleh stretched out on her side of the bed, but Faiga couldn't get comfortable. She knew exactly how to give the whole family a wonderful Yom Tov, but she couldn't figure out the right person to confide in.

"I wish Tzireleh and I were all grown up. Then we'd be best friends and I could tell her my plans," thought Faiga.

Faiga looked over at Tzireleh. *Well, maybe she's a little more grown up than I realized. I mean, she did know better than to stand under a tree during a storm.*

Faiga thought some more. *And, she worked really hard picking berries that day. Why, she picked almost as many as I did.*

Faiga's lips curled upward into a broad happy smile.

Would Tzireleh be a helpful partner? There was only one way to find out.

"Pssst, Tzireleh, wake up! I have something exciting to tell you! We're going to surprise Mama and Papa and everybody!"

* * *

As the days past and Yom Tov drew closer, it seemed that the two sisters would burst with excitement. They were forever whispering and laughing together, bubbling with anticipation.

Once Faiga had told Tzireleh about the new plan, the little girl couldn't do enough to help.

They had gathered all the tools they needed for the hyssop harvest and stashed everything in the barn.

Tzireleh even scrubbed the wheelbarrow so they'd have a clean place to put the precious flowers.

The only important thing Faiga couldn't figure out was where to plant the hyssop.

Near the house? Everyone would see it. Near the barn? It wouldn't be safe from the animals. Near the road? It could easily get trampled.

One morning, Tzireleh came in from the garden with a basket of beets. Her eyes were shining.

"Faiga, meet me behind the chicken coops. I have a surprise for you!"

Faiga finished dressing the baby and put him gently in his cradle. Quietly she slipped outside to meet her sister.

Tzireleh was pacing back and forth, her face wild with joy.

"Look!" she pointed. "That's the perfect spot!"

Behind the chicken coops lay a patch of Mama's garden where nothing but weeds grew. She hadn't had a chance to plant more vegetables this season, so that one whole corner lay neglected.

"Tzireleh, you're brilliant!" Faiga took her sister's hands, and they did a happy little dance. "There's a fence around it; nobody comes here – that's it! Tomorrow, let's go get our hyssop!"

* * *

That evening, while Tzireleh went out to feed the chickens, Mama started to wash the dishes. Faiga went over to help. She took a deep breath; this was her chance. She had to get permission to go back into the forest.

"Mama," Faiga began.

"Yes?" Mama said absently.

"After chores tomorrow, could Tzireleh and I go looking for berries again?"

Her mother frowned. Faiga could tell when Mama was about to say no.

"I'd be much more careful, really. And I heard Papa say how clear the skies looked. I don't think we'd be caught in the rain this time. Please?"

Mama didn't answer right away.

"We'd go earlier and be back earlier... I..."

This wasn't coming out the way Faiga had hoped.

"Oh, Mama... don't you trust me?"

Mama turned and wiped her hands on her apron. She looked at Faiga for what seemed like a long time.

"You know I do, maideleh. It's just that I worry about you and want you to be safe."

She pulled Faiga into a tight hug. Faiga hugged back, feeling warm and loved and protected. Finally she let go and looked into Mama's face.

"So, can we go?"

Mama smiled. "Yes, after your chores and not a minute sooner."

Faiga waved the dishcloth over her head. Victory! With Hashem's help, the esrog wallet, the tzedakah wallet, and Papa's pockets would all be full!

Chapter Seven

Harvesting the Hyssop

Faiga was so excited she could barely sleep that night. She kept looking out the window to see if it was time to start the morning chores.

She couldn't wait to get all that lovely hyssop just waiting for her in the forest.

Even before Papa woke up, the two girls were dressed, had davened and were ready to go. Tzireleh yawned and rubbed her eyes.

"Come on," Faiga urged. "I'll feed the chickens, and you milk Chiggy. I want to get an early start today."

"Won't Mama see us taking the wheelbarrow and other things along?" Tzireleh asked.

"I already hid it all behind the big tree near the path. Don't worry."

The girls flew to finish their work. They ate breakfast quickly, and kissed their Mama goodbye.

She bent down and looked into their eyes. "Now remember – stay together, don't get lost, and be back in time for supper."

"We will," they chorused.

They each carried a clean basket for berries as they marched toward the forest. Behind the big tree, under a few branches, Faiga had hidden the wheelbarrow, scissors, and shovel.

She pulled off the branches and gripped that handles of the wheelbarrow.

"Tzireleh," she said, "you carry the shovel, and then we can switch."

"At last," thought Faiga. "At last, we're off!"

They made their way along the path, enjoying the fresh air, the beautiful day, and the utter joy of sharing a wonderful secret.

"Let's get the berries first," suggested Faiga. "We can't come home without any berries or everyone will wonder what we've done all day."

Tzireleh skipped happily next to her big sister. "Good idea," she agreed.

Everything was going so well, the girls even enjoyed remembering their last awful trip to the forest.

"This is where you walked in circles and got us lost," Tzireleh teased.

"And this is where you started crying," Faiga reminded her.

When they reached the clearing, they both fell silent. The big tree that almost crashed onto them was still there, on its side.

Faiga looked at Tzireleh's golden head and breathed a sigh of relief that nothing had happened to her... to either of them.

"Come on," shouted Tzireleh. "Let's pick some berries!"

* * *

Berry picking would have been enough of a job for one morning. But today, it was just the beginning. The girls retraced their steps, looking for the hidden patch of hyssop flowers.

With two heavy baskets full of sweet ripe blackberries in the wheelbarrow, Faiga couldn't walk very fast.

"Hurry," urged Tzireleh. "Do you remember where it is?"

"I don't know," Faiga said wearily, looking around. The rain had produced so much new growth in the forest that she had trouble recognizing the right way to go.

Faiga stopped to wipe her forehead and shake out her sore fingers. Blisters were forming from pushing the wheelbarrow. She felt hot and tired and a bit dizzy.

"I'm stopping at the river to cool off. Then we'll try to figure it out."

The two sisters sat down on the riverbank and dangled their hands in the rushing water. Faiga washed her face and lay down in the soft grass at the river's edge. She must have fallen asleep for a few minutes, because the next thing she knew, Tzireleh was shaking her awake.

"Enough resting, Faiga; it's getting late. Let's go!"

Faiga couldn't understand why she felt so slow and lazy all of a sudden. She made a brachah, drank some cool water, and stood up.

"I know what to do. Let's walk straight back from this triangle rock to find the tree I climbed last time. Right next to that tree was the patch of purple hyssop flowers that I picked to put in your hair."

Tzireleh smiled. "I want to push the wheelbarrow now," she insisted. Faiga was only too glad to give that job to her sister.

Slowly they made their way back through the forest.

"Faiga, look," Tzireleh pointed straight ahead. "There's the tree... that's it!"

The patch of purple flowers growing in the clearing was the most beautiful sight the girls had ever seen. How they had planned and prepared for this moment!

Tzireleh began running toward the hyssop, but Faiga stopped her.

"Oh, no you don't. Cover your hands with your sleeves as you walk, and watch out for poison ivy!"

Faiga pushed ferns and branches out of the way so Tzireleh could bring the wheelbarrow in as close as possible. Without wasting any time, Faiga began carefully shoveling large clods of earth from under the plants. Tzireleh tugged gently to remove each stalk with the roots. Then she placed each one in the wheelbarrow.

"That will pay for sugar and candy," the little girl sang out. She pulled out another plant. "This one will buy me a new hair ribbon. Let's get enough for the most beautiful esrog in the world!"

Faiga smiled at her younger sister's enthusiasm. They worked together so well; she could never have done this without Tzireleh! The girls laughed and talked as they gathered more and more hyssop.

As time went by, they both grew silent. There seemed to be no end to this job.

The day grew humid and hot. At first, Faiga tried to keep track of how many hyssop stalks they had harvested, but she soon lost count. Her blisters had burst and water ran down her aching hands and fingers.

"Faiga," Tzireleh said, "maybe we should stop. Your face is all red; we're both so tired. What do you think?"

"Let's get them all," Faiga grunted. "We won't have other chances to come back for more."

Shovel, tug... shovel, tug. Too tired to think, Faiga moved from one clump of flowers to another. Sweat poured down her face; Tzireleh's hair was full of leaves. This was back breaking work, but the girls kept going.

Finally Tzireleh sat down right on the ground. "Faiga, we have to stop now. Look! The wheelbarrow is full."

Faiga lifted her head and stared at the large pile of hyssop with amazement. They'd done it! They'd really done it.

No, Hashem had done it.

Faiga thought back over all the events of the past weeks. If her plans of selling babkas or berries had worked, she might have made a little bit of money, but never enough for all that her family needed... never as much as the hyssop was worth!

If they hadn't gotten lost in the forest, they never would have discovered the valuable purple flowers to begin with!

Smiling, Faiga handed Tzireleh the shovel and placed her cracked and bleeding hands on the wheelbarrow. Slowly, very slowly, the two sisters walked home.

They stashed the pile of hyssop in a cool corner of the barn and covered the roots with damp flour sacks.

Faiga stepped back to admire the harvest. "There. Now all we have to do is dry the flowers and plant the roots."

She and Tzireleh washed their hands and faces in a bucket of clean water by the door.

Then they each walked in holding a basket full of blackberries.

Mama was so happy to see the girls back safely. She was also a bit surprised when Faiga and Tzireleh went to sleep even earlier than their baby brother!

Chapter Eight
Trouble!

As Faiga slept, she had a strange dream. There she was, digging up hyssop in the forest, but every time she pulled up one plant, another one grew in its place. Faster and faster she dug, but there was no end in sight!

The hot sun beat down on Faiga's head; her hands were hurting; her back was sore. She groaned and wished for some cold water.

It was so hot, burning hot. Faiga moaned again. Suddenly, there was Mama, shaking her awake.

"Faiga, what is it? You were calling out in your sleep."

Faiga tried to sit up, but felt so dizzy that she fell back on the pillow. Mama put her cool hand on Faiga's forehead.

"Oh, maideleh... you're burning up with fever!"

In a few minutes, Papa came in and carried Tzireleh over to sleep in Mama's bed. Mama sat down next to Faiga and sponged her face and arms with cool water. Faiga started to shiver. Mama made some hot tea with honey and spooned some into her daughter's mouth, bit by bit.

Faiga couldn't look at the kerosene lamp in the corner; the light hurt her eyes. The room was spinning. She felt so hot, so sleepy, so thirsty.

Faiga dozed off and had the same dream... only this time, a huge tree was about to fall right on her! The frightened girl called out, "Mama!"

And Mama was right there, soothing her with cool water, singing *Roizenkes mit Mandlen*, until Faiga stopped thrashing and lay quietly.

But still, Faiga's fever climbed higher. Her breathing grew shallow and labored.

She felt the doctor examine her and listen to her heart, but had no strength to move or to open her eyes.

She heard the baby cry faintly, and her father's voice saying Tehillim, and then she slept again.

Faiga didn't even know if it was day or night. Sometimes shivering, other times too hot to stay under her blanket, all Faiga wanted to do was sleep.

* * *

Then, one morning, she opened her eyes and they didn't hurt. Too weak to sit up, Faiga said 'Modeh Ani' and looked around the room. Mama was dozing in a chair next to the bed.

The house was quiet and still. Where was everybody? How long had she been ill? Reluctant to wake Mama, Faiga lay in bed, waiting for something to happen.

In a little while, the door opened and Papa peeked in. Silently, he approached the bed and looked down at his daughter. Faiga smiled up at him, and watched his eyes widen with surprise, then fill with grateful tears.

"Boruch Hashem," he whispered, his voice husky. "Good morning, maideleh. How do you feel?"

"Hungry," Faiga croaked. Her voice sounded strange in her ears. "And curious. How long was I...?"

"It's been five days," answered Papa. "Five days of you so feverish, we didn't know what would happen." He stopped and cleared his throat.

Mama woke up from the sound. "What is it Yankel? What's wrong?"

"Boruch Hashem," Papa answered, "the fever broke; our Faiga's awake!"

Mama struggled to her feet, then did something Faiga had never seen her do before. She covered her face with her apron and sobbed.

"Mama," she begged, "please don't cry."

Mama bustled over and smiled at Faiga. "They're happy tears, maideleh. You had us all worried. Papa and I have done nothing but watch over you day and night. Let's get you into a fresh nightgown and you'll have some soup and toast."

Papa slipped quietly from the room. Faiga let Mama take care of her like a baby. Then she thought of something for the first time.

"Where are Tzireleh and the baby?"

Mama held a piece of bread over the fire with a fork. "They've been at your Aunt Taibke's ever since you got sick."

Faiga closed her eyes and sniffed the comforting smell of toasted bread. All at once, she thought of something else. The hyssop! What had happened to the precious plants stashed in the barn? Had Tzireleh forgotten about them? Were they moldy or dried out under the sacks? She had to find out!

"Mama, can Tzireleh come in to see me now?"

Mama smiled, delighted that Faiga was so much better and asking to see her sister. "Not yet, maideleh. You have to get your strength back first."

Tears formed in Faiga's eyes. "Please, Mama, I need to see her... just for a few minutes... please."

Mama brought the fragrant toast over to Faiga's bedside. "Shhhh, maideleh. Eat this and soon we'll see about guests."

Mama helped Faiga wash her hands, and then fed her bits of toast. When the plate was only half empty, Faiga was too tired to eat any more. She started to ask Mama if Tzireleh could come, but suddenly her eyelids felt too heavy to lift. Faiga leaned back into the pillow and slept... a deep, healing sleep.

* * *

When Faiga woke next, it was dark in the room. Papa sat in the chair next to her bed, an open sefer in his hand.

"Papa?" she whispered.

"I'm here, maideleh. Your mama had to get some rest. She's all worn out with caring for you. Shall I help you sit up?"

"Yes, please," answered Faiga.

Papa plumped the pillows and helped Faiga ease into a sitting position. Her head felt light and dizzy; she leaned back and took a few deep breaths.

Papa held a cup of well water to her lips, and Faiga made a brachah and let it trickle down her parched throat.

"Easy," Papa said. "A little at a time."

Faiga took a few more sips. "Papa?"

"Yes," he answered.

"When can Tzireleh come and see me?"

Papa's eyes twinkled. "You've missed her, haven't you?"

Faiga thought about that. She wanted to see Tzireleh to find out about the hyssop, but also because they'd grown so close.

"Why, yes," Faiga answered, sounding a bit surprised. "I do miss her."

"I thought so," answered Papa. "I always hoped you and Tzireleh would be good friends as well as sisters."

He held his fingers to his lips. "I have a little surprise for you, Faiga."

Tiptoeing to the door, he opened it a crack and nodded his head. All at once, Faiga saw a familiar figure stepping hesitantly into the room. Tzireleh!

The little girl looked pale and frightened until she saw Faiga sitting up and smiling at her.

"Faiga? Are you better?"

Faiga nodded and held out her arms; Tzireleh perched on the bed and gave her sister a squeeze.

Papa stood beaming at the two of them, so Faiga whispered quietly into Tzireleh's ear, "What happened to...?"

Mama's voice interrupted the scene. "Yankel! Is Tzireleh in there?"

Papa shrugged his shoulders. "It's just that Faiga wanted to see her so badly..."

Mama laughed. "As soon as I close my eyes for one minute, this sickroom becomes a party!"

Faiga could see Mama wasn't upset. Glad to have them together again, she pulled both girls into a warm hug.

"That's really enough for now," Papa said. "Come, Tzireleh. Faiga needs to eat and rest and grow strong."

Faiga almost groaned out loud as her parents led Tzireleh out of the room. When would she ever find out what had happened to all their hard work? Suddenly, her eyelids drooped. Faiga stretched out and slept, dreaming of fields of purple hyssop.

* * *

Two weeks passed. Mama and Papa watched over her carefully, afraid of a setback. The children were home again, but they hadn't been allowed in to disturb Faiga's rest. Tzireleh came in for a short visit each day, but always, one of her parents remained in the room, hovering nearby.

Faiga simply didn't have an opportunity to find out what she was aching to know. What had happened to the hyssop? If the roots had dried out, at least they could still sell the flowers to Shaya for his spice shop. Yom Tov was almost here; there wasn't much time.

Faiga churned with impatience. Today her parents were going to let her come out of the room for the first time and sit in the kitchen by the fire.

She lay on the bed, wearing her warm robe over her flannel nightgown. She wiggled her feet impatiently, waiting for Mama to help her.

"Here we are," Mama smiled. Her eyes looked bright with excitement as she helped Faiga stand next to the bed.

Faiga was anxious to walk on her own, but she still needed to lean on Mama. Concentrating, she took small, wobbly steps toward the kitchen.

The door swung open! To her joy, the entire family stood there to greet her... Papa, holding Mendeleh, Tzireleh standing proudly next to Aunt Taibke and Uncle Getzel.

A chair near the fire was waiting for her, and Faiga sank into it gratefully. Tzireleh covered her big sister with a warm winter shawl, and Papa placed little Mendeleh on Faiga's lap.

She sighed with contentment. Her eyes took in all the familiar, comforting objects in the room... and then spotted some not-so-familiar items.

Was that an esrog-sized box on top of the highest shelf? Faiga stared.

The kitchen pantry shelves were full. A large sack of flour stood in the corner. Then she noticed a jar full of white sugar and a dish of candy on the table.

Faiga glanced down. Tzireleh was wearing a beautiful pair of leather shoes, stiff and shiny and brand new.

She gazed quizzically at her younger sister. "But how did you ever...?"

Tzireleh laughed and everybody joined in. "Surprise, Faiga!"

Papa beamed at her. "Oh, maideleh, thanks to your hard work, we have an esrog and everything we need for Yom Tov... and enough to give away for tzedakah!"

Tzireleh chimed in, "I realized that I needed everyone's help to dry the hyssop and plant the roots, but I knew it could still be a surprise for someone... and that someone was you, Faiga! You helped make your very own surprise!"

Faiga laughed and reached for Tzireleh's hand. A younger sister really could be a good friend!

Mama went into her room and came back holding a blue silk dress perfect for an eleven-year-old girl.

Speechless with wonder, Faiga gazed at the rich color, the ruffled hem and the beautiful lace collar.

"Rabbi Glick has invited us all to a certain wedding in two week's time," smiled Mama. "Your old Shabbos dress is just the right size for Tzireleh now, so you're the only one who needed something new to wear. Will this do?"

Faiga caught her breath. That elegant dress was hers!

"Oh, Mama," she stammered. "Thank you... thank you, everybody!"

Faiga looked around gratefully at the faces of her loving family. She knew she would remember this wonderful moment as long as she lived.

Full of joy, she whispered, "Thank You, Hashem, for helping me and showing me the way."

Faiga's Babke Recipe

Dough:

¾ cup warm (not hot) water with a drop of
honey mixed in

¾ cup honey

2 teaspoons dry yeast

1 egg

2 tablespoons oil

1 pinch salt

3 ½ cups flour

(1 egg beaten with 1 tablespoon honey for
crust)

Filling:

1 cup honey (or more to spread on rolled
out dough)

½ cup cinnamon

4 tablespoons flour

1 teaspoon water

Preheat oven to 325 degrees. Dissolve yeast in warm water with drop of honey. In a separate bowl, mix honey, oil, egg, and salt. Combine with yeast. Add flour and mix.

Roll out dough to ½ inch thick in a triangle shape. Smear generously with honey and spread ¾ of the cinnamon, flour and water mixture (should be crumbly).

Roll the bottom of the triangle in a tight roll, towards the point.

Bring the ends of the roll together to form a ring.

Spread with beaten egg mixed with honey. Sprinkle with the rest of the filling mixture.

Bake at 325 degrees for 1 hour until golden brown, or until a toothpick comes out clean.

(Please note: Honey is not to be served to babies under one year of age.)

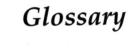

Glossary

Glossary:

Amein – Amen

Aravos – Willow branches used on Sukkos

Bais Hamikdosh – Holy Temple

Brachah – Blessing

Challah – Sabbath loaf

Davened – Prayed

Esrog (Esrogim pl.) – Citron(s) used on Sukkos

Haddassim – Myrtle branches used on Sukkos

Hashem – G-d

Im Yirtzeh Hashem – G-d willing

Kallah – Bride

Kapital – Chapter

L'hafrish Challah – To Separate Challah

Lulov – Palm branch

Maideleh (Maidelach pl.) – "Little girl," a term of endearment

Mitzvah – One of 613 Commandments in the Torah, good deed

Modeh Ani – Morning prayer of thanksgiving

"Roizenkes mit Mandlen" – "Raisins and Almonds," a famous lullabye

Rosh Hashanah – New Year

Sefer – Holy book

Shema – The 'Hear O Israel' Prayer

Shul – Synagogue

Simchas Torah – Holiday of rejoicing with the Torah

Sukkah – Temporary dwelling or booth in which all meals are eaten on Sukkos

Sukkos – Festival of Booths

Tefillah – Prayer

Tehillim – Psalms

Teshuvah – Repentence

Torah – The Law and wisdom contained in the Jewish Scripture and Oral Tradition; The Five Books of Moses

Tzedakah – Charity

Yom Kippur – Day of Atonement

Yom Tov – Holiday

'Zol zein a kaparah' – 'May it be an atonement'

Books in the Fun-to-Read Series

Making Jewish History Fun-to Read!